Tom and Ricky
and the
Red Hot Rod

Bob Wright

High Noon Books
Novato, California

Cover Design: Nancy Peach
Interior Illustrations: Herb Heidinger

International Standard Book Number: 0-87879-329-1

7 6 5 4 3 2 1 0 9 8
20 19 18 17 16 15 14 13 12 11

Contents

CHAPTER 1

A Hot Saturday

Tom stopped his bike. He was in front of Ricky's house. But he didn't see Ricky.

"Ricky! Ricky!" he called.

Ricky didn't call back to him.

Patches was in the house. He started to bark. He could hear Tom.

"Stop barking, Patches," Ricky said. He didn't hear Tom. He just heard Patches barking.

Patches looked at Ricky. He could hear Tom. Why couldn't Ricky hear him?

Tom called again, "Ricky! Ricky!"

Patches barked again. But this time Ricky could hear Tom.

"Now I know why you barked," Ricky said.

Ricky went to the front door. "Come on in, Tom," he said.

Tom left his bike by the door.

"What are you doing today?" Tom asked.

"I have to clean my room," Ricky said. "Why? Want to do something?"

"How about riding around?" Tom asked.

"I can go if you help me," Ricky answered.

"OK. But let's hurry," Tom said.

They went to Ricky's room. It didn't take much time to clean it up. They put things away.

Very soon the room looked good.

"That was fast," Ricky said.

"OK. Let's go," Tom said.

"Where do you want to go?" Ricky asked.

"We could ride to the park," Tom said.

"OK. I can go but I can't stay out too long. I have to help my dad when he gets home," Ricky said.

"How about Patches? Can he go, too?" Tom asked.

"Patches will like it. He can run around in the park with us," Ricky said.

Patches sat up. He knew they were talking about him. He wagged his tail. He liked going with them.

Ricky called out to his mother, "I'll be back in about two hours."

"Don't be longer than that. We have things to do today," she called back.

"Boy, it's hot. There will be a lot of people in the park today," Tom said.

Ricky got his bike. Tom was waiting for him in front of the house.

They started for the park. It would be fun to ride around for two hours. Patches ran along with them.

The park wasn't very far from Ricky's house. It didn't take long to get there.

As they got near the park, a red hot rod went by them. Two men were in the front seat.

The red hot rod was going very fast.

"Did you see that hot rod? There were two men in it. They could have hit us," Ricky said.

"They must be in a hurry," Tom said.

"Look. They are going into the park," Ricky said.

"They better slow down. They could hurt someone," Tom said.

CHAPTER 2

A Fast Car

It was a hot day. A lot of people were in the park. People wanted to play and eat there.

Tom and Ricky wanted to stop to rest. Every place they looked there were people.

Then Ricky saw some grass near some big trees. It was near the road. It was a small place. There were not too many people there.

"Let's stop over there and rest. Then we'll get going again," Ricky said.

They stopped and got off their bikes.

"Look," Tom said, "there's that red hot rod again."

"They are still going fast," Ricky said.

"They are going to hit someone," Tom said.

The car went by Tom and Ricky. Patches barked. A bag fell out of the car as it went by them.

"What was that?" Tom asked.

"I don't know. It fell out of the hot rod," Ricky said.

"It looked like a bag," Tom said.

The bag landed on the grass near Tom and Ricky. Patches saw it, too.

"Come on. Let's see what it is," Ricky said.

They all ran over to the bag. Patches got there first. He grabbed the bag and ran with it into the trees.

The bag landed on the grass. Patches saw it, too.

"Patches! Come here," Ricky called.

Patches didn't come back.

"We'll have to go and get him," Ricky said.

"I wonder what is in the bag," Tom said.

"I don't know. Maybe Patches thinks it has bones in it," Ricky said.

Tom and Ricky started to walk to the trees. Then they saw Patches coming back. He didn't have the bag. He was wagging his tail.

"Where did you put that bag, Patches?" Ricky asked.

Patches didn't move. He just sat and looked at Ricky.

"He thinks we're playing a game," Ricky said. "Let's see if we can find it."

Tom and Ricky went to the trees. There were many trees and many rocks. The bag could be anywhere.

"I bet he hid it," Ricky said.

"Patches. This isn't a game. Where's the bag?" Tom said.

Patches just kept walking with Tom and Ricky.

"Well, maybe there wasn't anything in that bag. Come on. Let's go," Ricky said.

"Let's try one more time. Patches, get the bag for us," Tom said.

Patches didn't do anything. He just sat down and looked at Tom.

"OK. Let's go," Tom said.

They went back to their bikes.

Just then Ricky looked at the road. "Look. There's that hot rod again."

"But it isn't going fast this time," Tom said.

They looked at the red hot rod. It pulled up and stopped next to them.

CHAPTER 3

The Two Men

One of the men called to Tom and Ricky. He looked mad. "Did you see a bag? We dropped it out of our car about ten minutes ago. We think we lost it somewhere near here."

"It might be over in the trees," Ricky said.

"How did it get over there?" the other man said.

Tom said, "Our dog saw it. He ran over to it. Then he took it to the trees."

"We play games like that," Ricky said.

"Patches hides things. Then we try to find them," Tom said.

The man turned to the other man. "The dog took it. He took the bag," he said.

"What's your name, kid?" the man asked.

"I'm Ricky. Patches is my dog. This is Tom," Ricky said.

"I'm Ed. This is Bill. We'll give you five dollars if you can find that bag," Ed said.

"Maybe the dog can find it," Bill said.

"We went looking for it. We saw Patches get it and take it into the trees. We couldn't find it," Ricky said.

"Come on. Let's all go and look for the bag," Bill said.

Ed and Bill got out of the car. "Show us where your dog went," Bill said.

"You have a nice car. I'd like to have one like that some day," Tom said.

"Sure, sure. Let's just look for the bag," Bill said.

Ed and Bill walked fast. "Come on. Show us where your dog went. We don't have a lot of time," Ed said.

"He walked over to the trees. We don't know where he went after that," Ricky said.

"How long was he there?" Bill asked.

"Not very long," Tom said.

"Why do you want the bag back?" Ricky asked.

"We didn't mean to drop it out of the car. We forgot we put something in it. Now we want it back," Ed said.

"Stop talking. Let's look for that bag," Bill said.

Tom and Ricky walked with Patches. Ed and Bill were in back of them. They looked for all the places Patches might have dug a hole. They found some little holes and some big ones. But the bag wasn't in any of them.

Bill started to get mad. "We have things to do. We want that bag. Make your dog find it," he said.

Patches looked at Bill. He started to bark. He didn't like Bill and Ed.

Ricky didn't like it when Bill got mad. They wanted Patches to think it was a game. Then he would get the bag. He didn't like Ed and Bill so he didn't get the bag.

"Where did you hide the bag, Patches?" Ricky asked.

Patches just sat where he was. He didn't move. He barked at Ed and Bill.

"Patches is my dog. We play a game like this at home," Ricky said.

"Well, make him find that bag," Ed said.

"He won't do it. He wants us to find it," Ricky said.

Patches didn't move. He was waiting for Ricky to find the bag.

"Find that bag," Bill yelled.

Tom and Ricky didn't like what was going on. They wanted to go.

Ed started to kick Patches. Bill grabbed him. "Stop. Look over there."

Tom and Ricky looked. There was a police car. It stopped next to the bikes.

"Nice dog," Ed said. Now he was trying to be nice.

CHAPTER 4

The Police Car

The policeman saw Tom and Ricky and the two men. He got out of his car. He walked over to them.

"Can I help you?" he said. "You look like you need some help."

"We're just looking for something we lost," Bill said.

"Patches took their bag and hid it. We saw it fall out of their car," Ricky said.

"We don't know where he put it," Tom said.

"Whose bag is it?" the policeman asked.

Ed and Bill looked at each other.

"We dropped it out of our car," Bill said.

"Whose bag is it?" the policeman asked.
Ed and Bill looked at each other.

"Then we came back to get it," Ed said.

"But it was gone," Bill said.

"What was in the bag?" the policeman asked.

"Not too much. We don't need it after all," Bill said.

"I think we'll be going," Ed said.

"Are you sure you don't need the bag?" the policeman asked.

"We can keep on looking for the bag," Ricky said to the policeman.

"If we find the bag, tell us where to call you," the policeman said to Ed and Bill.

"That's OK. It was nothing. We don't need it," Bill said.

"We don't have time to stay here," Ed said.

"We have to see some people," Bill said.

Ed and Bill started to walk away. Patches barked at them. He started to walk after them. He kept on barking.

"Patches, come here," Ricky called.

Patches just kept walking after the two men.

The policeman turned to talk to Tom and Ricky. "Now, tell me again about that bag. What's that all about?"

"We were here on the grass. The men went by in their red hot rod," Tom said.

"Red hot rod?" the policeman said.

"Yes. They dropped the bag. Patches got it and took it into the trees. He hid it there," Ricky said.

“Then those two men came,” Tom said. “They said they wanted the bag.”

“They were mad,” Ricky said.

“Patches knows where the bag is. He thinks this is a game,” Tom said.

“A game?” the policeman asked.

“We play a game at home. Patches hides something. I have to find it,” Ricky said.

“Some money was taken from the bank near here. People said two men got away in a red hot rod. Maybe there was money in that bag. Stay here,” the policeman said.

The policeman ran to look for Ed and Bill. The red hot rod wasn’t there. And Patches was gone, too.

The policeman came back. "They left," he said. "I'm going to try to get them."

Ricky turned to Tom. "Where's Patches?" he asked.

Tom and Ricky both called for Patches. He didn't come.

"I think they took your dog," the policeman said. "Stay here. I will come back." The policeman left.

CHAPTER 5

Patches is Missing

Tom and Ricky didn't know why Ed and Bill took Patches. The policeman told them to stay right there. They waited by their bikes.

"Ricky, do you think they will hurt Patches?" Tom asked.

"No. I think they will come back. And they will bring Patches with them. They want that bag," Ricky said.

"They said they didn't want it," Tom said.

"I think they do want it," Ricky said.

"Do you think there is something in it they need?" Tom asked.

"Yes, I do. First they dropped it from the car. Then they came back to look for it. Then they left and said they didn't need it. Then they took Patches. They need Patches. They will be back," Ricky said.

"Then if there is something in the bag, they have to find it before anyone else does," Tom said.

"That's right. So let's sit down and wait here," Ricky said.

Tom and Ricky sat down on the grass. They waited for the policeman to come back. In a little while they heard a dog barking.

"I think I hear Patches," Tom said.

"There are a lot of people in the park today. Lots of them have dogs," Ricky said.

"But it sounds like Patches," Tom said.

They looked over to the trees.

"Look, Tom," Ricky said.

They got down low.

"It's Patches. I can see him. He has a rope around his neck," Tom said.

"I can see Ed. He's holding the rope. He's making Patches walk all around the trees. I bet he thinks Patches will show him where the bag is," Ricky said.

"That way they can get the bag and then get away with it," Tom said.

"Where's the policeman and where's the red hot rod?" Ricky asked.

"I bet they left the red hot rod where no one could see it," Tom said.

"And then they walked back here with Patches," Ricky said.

"What should we do?" Tom asked.

"I can call Patches," Ricky said.

"No. Don't do that. Then they will know we're here," Tom said.

I just don't want them to hurt Patches," Ricky said.

"As long as Patches keeps looking for the bag, he is OK," Tom said.

"Where's that policeman?" Ricky asked.

Just then they saw the police car. The policeman had come back. Tom and Ricky were glad to see him.

CHAPTER 6

Help Comes

Tom and Ricky got up. They tried to stay low so Ed and Bill wouldn't see them. They got to the police car as fast as they could.

The policeman got out of the car. "I found the red hot rod. It is near here. But I didn't see the two men," the policeman said.

"They came back here," Tom said.

"Where are they now?" he asked.

"They went back over to the trees. They have Patches with them," Tom said.

"Did they see you?" the policeman asked.

"We don't think they did. We tried to stay low," Ricky said.

"That's good thinking," the policeman said.

"They have a rope on Patches. They are making him look for that bag," Tom said.

"I think I know what's going on," the policeman said.

Tom and Ricky looked at him. "What's going on?" Ricky asked.

"The bank was held up. I just found out that two men did it. They left in a red hot rod," he said.

"Do you think those men with Patches are the two men?" Ricky asked.

"It sure looks like it," he said.

"What should we do?" Tom asked.

"I need to get help," he said.

"The bank was held up. They left in a red hot rod," the policeman said.

The policeman got back into his car. He called in for more police. Then he got back out of the car. "Those men may hurt someone. They want to get that bag. Don't go near the trees. Stay right here."

"How much money did they take from the bank?" Tom asked.

"There is a lot of money in that bag," the policeman said. "That's why they want to get it."

"What are you going to do?" Ricky asked.

"We'll stay here. The other police are coming. Some will go to the red hot rod. The others will come here. There are a lot of people here in the park today. We don't want anyone to get hurt," the policeman said.

Two other police cars came. They didn't park near Tom and Ricky.

"If people see too many police cars, it won't be good. That is why they are not parking near us," the policeman said.

The policeman walked over to the other policemen. They talked for a minute. Then they called Tom and Ricky.

"We have a plan. This is what we will do," the policeman said.

CHAPTER 7

Patches Gets Away

The policeman told Tom and Ricky what to do.

"We don't want anyone to get hurt. We think this will work. Do you want to help us?" he asked.

"Yes, tell us what to do," Ricky said.

"OK. We will stay here. Walk back over to your bikes. Then call Patches. Do you think he will come to you?" the policeman asked.

"Yes, he will come," Ricky said.

"What about that rope?" Tom asked.

"I think Patches can move fast. He can pull away from it," Ricky said.

"OK, then. Let's try it," the policeman said.

Tom and Ricky walked back to their bikes.

Then they started to call Patches. Patches could hear them, but he couldn't see them. He knew they were near. He looked around.

Ed turned to Bill. "It's those boys. They're calling the dog."

"But we still need that bag," Bill said.

"Maybe they'll go away if the dog doesn't do anything," Ed said.

Patches started to bark. "Shut up," Bill said.

Patches barked some more.

Tom and Ricky kept on calling for Patches.

Then, all of a sudden, Patches started to run. He moved so fast that the rope was pulled away from Ed. Patches ran to Tom and Ricky. The rope was still around his neck.

"Now what do we do?" Ed asked.

"Let's get back to the car," Bill said. "We can come back again and look for the money."

They started to run to the red hot rod.

All of a sudden they saw the police. "Stop where you are. Put your hands in the air," the police said.

Ed and Bill stopped. They had their hands up in the air.

"Don't do anything. We're taking you in," the policeman said.

"We didn't do anything," Ed said.

"We were just looking for our bag. We lost it, and that dog took it and hid it," Bill said.

Then, all of a sudden, Patches started to run. The rope was pulled away from Ed.

"That bag had money in it. You took that money from the bank, didn't you?" the policeman said.

"We're not saying anything," Ed said.

The policeman read them their rights. Then they took them away.

CHAPTER 8

The Surprise

The police took Ed and Bill away. Tom and Ricky took the rope off Patches.

The policeman came back. "I need your names. And tell me where you live," he said.

Tom and Ricky told him what he needed to know. Then the policeman said, "I wish we could find that bag. We need to get that money. Ed and Bill could go free if we don't find it."

"Patches, we need your help," Ricky said.

Patches looked at Ricky.

"Come on, Patches. Show us where the bag is," Tom said.

Patches just sat. He looked at Tom and then at Ricky. Then all of a sudden, he ran back to the trees. They all ran after him.

Patches ran right to some rocks. He started to dig.

Ricky called out, "Look. There's the bag. I can see it."

Tom moved the rocks out of the way. "Here it is," he said.

Tom gave the bag to the policeman. The policeman opened it up. "Look," he said, "here's the money."

"We have what we need," the policeman said.

"Patches, we're going to give you a bone for helping out," Ricky said.

Ricky called out, "Look. There's the bag."

“Give him a big one,” the policeman said. “Without Patches we would not have found the money.”

Patches seemed happy. He knew he had helped a lot.

“I’ll come to your house tomorrow,” the policeman said.

Tom and Ricky got on their bikes and went back to Ricky’s house.

The next day the policeman came by. Tom was at Ricky’s house.

“These two men won’t be holding up any more banks for a while,” he said. “People at the bank said they were the ones who took the money. They also saw the red hot rod.”

"But why did they drop the bag out of the car?" Ricky asked.

"They thought the police were after them. They wanted to get rid of the money. When they knew the police weren't in back of them, they came back to get it. Thanks to Patches, they didn't find it," the policeman said.

Patches wagged his tail.

"Here is something for you, Patches," the policeman said.

He had a bag. He opened it up and started to laugh.

"Tom, look at this," Ricky said.

Tom looked in the bag and started to laugh.

Then Ricky took out a big bone for Patches.

"That's for helping us, Patches. And thanks, Tom and Ricky, for your help," he said.

Patches took the bone and ran out into the yard.

"I'll bet he's going to hide it," Tom said.

They all laughed.